Dear Parents and Educators,

Welcome to Penguin Young Readers! As parents and educators, you know that each child develops at his or her own pace—in terms of speech, critical thinking, and, of course, reading. Penguin Young Readers recognizes this fact. As a result, each Penguin Young Readers book is assigned a traditional easy-to-read level (1–4) as well as a Guided Reading Level (A–P). Both of these systems will help you choose the right book for your child. Please refer to the back of each book for specific leveling information. Penguin Young Readers features esteemed authors and illustrators, stories about favorite characters, fascinating nonfiction, and more!

When Tiny Was Tiny

LEVEL 1

GUIDED
READING
LEVEL **D**

This book is perfect for an **Emergent Reader** who:
* can read in a left-to-right and top-to-bottom progression;
* can recognize some beginning and ending letter sounds;
* can use picture clues to help tell the story; and
* can understand the basic plot and sequence of simple stories.

Here are some **activities** you can do during and after reading this book:
* Compare/Contrast: When Tiny is a tiny puppy, he fits in a shoe. But when he grows up, he is too big to fit in his doghouse! Discuss how Tiny the puppy is different from Tiny the big dog. How is he the same?
* Sight Words: Sight words are frequently used words that readers must know just by looking at them. These words are known instantly, on sight. Knowing these words helps children develop into efficient readers. As you read the story, point out the sight words that are listed below.

big	could	for	he	in	my	run	still	to
can	did	get	here	is	not	said	the	was
come	does	good	him	me	now	some	this	when

Remember, sharing the love of reading with a child is the best gift you can give!

—Bonnie Bader, EdM
  Penguin Young Readers program

*Penguin Young Readers are leveled by independent reviewers applying the standards developed by Irene Fountas and Gay Su Pinnell in *Matching Books to Readers: Using Leveled Books in Guided Reading*, Heinemann, 1999.

For Samson, the best dog in the whole world,
and for Tim, who was there at the start—CM

To my beautiful mom who nurtured
my creative gift since birth and who prayed
me into God's kingdom. I love you!—RD

Penguin Young Readers
Published by the Penguin Group
Penguin Group (USA) Inc., 375 Hudson Street, New York, New York 10014, USA
Penguin Group (Canada), 90 Eglinton Avenue East, Suite 700, Toronto, Ontario M4P 2Y3, Canada
(a division of Pearson Penguin Canada Inc.)
Penguin Books Ltd., 80 Strand, London WC2R 0RL, England
Penguin Group Ireland, 25 St. Stephen's Green, Dublin 2, Ireland (a division of Penguin Books Ltd.)
Penguin Group (Australia), 250 Camberwell Road, Camberwell, Victoria 3124, Australia
(a division of Pearson Australia Group Pty. Ltd.)
Penguin Books India Pvt. Ltd., 11 Community Centre, Panchsheel Park, New Delhi—110 017, India
Penguin Group (NZ), 67 Apollo Drive, Rosedale, Auckland 0632, New Zealand
(a division of Pearson New Zealand Ltd.)
Penguin Books (South Africa) (Pty.) Ltd., 24 Sturdee Avenue,
Rosebank, Johannesburg 2196, South Africa

Penguin Books Ltd., Registered Offices: 80 Strand, London WC2R 0RL, England

Text copyright © 1999 by Cari Meister. Illustrations copyright © 1999 by Rich Davis.
All rights reserved. First published in 1999 by Viking and Puffin Books, imprints of Penguin Group
(USA) Inc. Published in 2012 by Penguin Young Readers, an imprint of Penguin Group (USA) Inc.,
345 Hudson Street, New York, New York 10014. Manufactured in China.

The Library of Congress has catalogued the Viking edition
under the following Control Number: 98047827

ISBN 978-0-14-130419-9   10 9 8

When Tiny Was Tiny

WITHDRAWN

by Cari Meister
illustrated by Rich Davis

Penguin Young Readers
An Imprint of Penguin Group (USA) Inc.

This is Tiny.

This is Tiny when he was tiny.

He fit in my shoe.

He fit in my bag.

He fit in my pocket.

Tiny did not stay tiny.

Tiny grew.

Now Tiny is not tiny.

Now Tiny is very big!

When Tiny was tiny, he dug in
the dirt.

He still does.

When Tiny was tiny,

he licked me.

He still does. Yuck!

When Tiny was tiny,

he had big feet.

He still does. Ow!

Get off my foot, Tiny.

Some days Tiny thinks he is

still tiny.

I try to teach him.

I tell him he is not tiny.

I tell him he is big.

I tell him big is good.

When Tiny was tiny, he could

not run fast.

Now he can.

Wait for me, Tiny!

When Tiny was tiny, he could
not do tricks.

Now he can.

Good dog, Tiny!

When Tiny was tiny, he was

my best friend.

He still is.